Getting A Job

"C'mon, Mike!" Macey told me. "You can't sit on this couch forever!"

"Yes I can!" I replied without taking my eyes off the TV.

She stood in front of the TV to try and block it.

"You really think you're going to make money by watching TV all day?" she asked.

"I'm sure it's possible somewhere," I said while adjusting my head to look around her.

"Well, it's not possible here!"

She then shut off the TV and bent down to look at me eye-to-eye.

"Look," she said in a serious tone.

"When you dropped out of high school, I promised Mom I'd make sure you had a successful life."

"I know," I told her without really caring.

"And you're not going to get anywhere in life if you don't try and get a job somewhere!"

"Mace, you know me; I'm, not really a hard working guy!"

"I know, but as your big sister, I have to keep you motivated to do

Five Nights At Freddy's

your best!"

"You don't really have to, you know."

"I know, but a Schmidt never fails. Mom got really pissed when you dropped out, but maybe you could make it up to her by trying to get your life back together!"

I then deeply sighed. I hated working, but I hate disappointing Mom even more.

"Fine," I said. "I'll look through the paper and find out who's offering jobs."

"That's the spirit!" She said with a smile.

She then went into the bathroom to take her evening shower.

I really didn't know what I was thinking when I decided to quit school, but I didn't think it would be like this. I have no money, my parents are upset, and I'm living with my sister in her apartment! I really hit rock bottom. It really didn't help I didn't like physical labor, but I got to do what I got to do.

So I went over to today's paper (Macey conveniently left it on the kitchen table), and I looked through the Want Ads.

I saw job listings for cashiers, drivers, supply stockers, and other stuff. None of the, were really up my alley. I then threw the paper on the table with frustration. When I did, Macey got out of the bathroom with towels wrapped around her body and hair.

"Find anything?" She asked as she took the towel off her hair and started drying it.

Five Nights At Freddy's

"Nothing I feel like I can do," I said with a groan, to which she sighed in frustration.

"There's got to be SOMETHING even you can do," she said as she picked up the paper.

She flipped through some things before stopping and appearing to read an Ad.

"How about this?" she asked as she grabbed a red Sharpie from the table and drew a circle in the paper.

She then gave it to me and I looked at what was circled. The first thing I saw what looked like a giant teddy bear with a top hat and bow tie, as well as giant blew eyes.

Next to it read the following:

HELP WANTED! Freddy Fazbear's Pizza. Family pizzeria looking for security guard to work the night shift.

Monday's through Fridays, 12 am to 6 am.

Monitor cameras, insure safety of equipment and animatronic characters.

Not responsible for injury/dismemberment.

$120 a week.

"Sounds simple enough for you," she told me. "Looks like you just got to watch the security cameras."

Five Nights At Freddy's

I was just still staring at the ad with confusion.

"What's this about dismemberment?" I asked, not expecting her to know the answer.

She took the paper back from me and read it again.

"Maybe it's just a legal thing," she said with a shrug. "You know, if the worst happened.

"I guess, but it's only $120 a week! That's like $4 and hour!"

"Wow! And here I thought you didn't know how to do math!"

"Oh, shut up!"

"Ok, so it's not the best money," she continued, "but is there any other job you would want to have here?"

She got me there.

"Fine," I told her, taking the paper back. "I'll call them and ask about the job."

"Thank you," she said. "And if it helps, don't feel like you have to do this for money. Do it for Mom and Dad. Ok?"

"Ok..."

She then smiled and went into her bedroom.

I groaned and dialed the number. I didn't want a job, but I didn't have a choice. Though to be honest, this didn't seem like a difficult job.

Five Nights At Freddy's
Interview

Well, needless to say, they were interested in me, despite my educational and work background. I was asked to meet with the boss on Sunday afternoon to discuss some things like what I'd have to do and stuff. So I agreed. Not like I had a choice.

I drove over there and got my first good look at the place. The exterior was big and colorful, with a giant sign reading FREDDY FAZBEAR'S PIZZA in giant red letter.

I went inside and was instantly greeted by tons of little children running around. A good majority of them were by some sort of stage, where I could see three animatronic animals singing a cheesy tune.

The one in the middle, holding the microphone, was the bear I had seen in the advertisement. To his right was a lavender bunny playing a red electric guitar and to his left was a yellow duck-looking thing playing a keyboard. They all looked really creepy and old, but the kids seem to love them anyway.

I then made my way around the place and found the manager's office. I knocked on the open door and the manager looked up from his paperwork.

"Ah! You must be Mike Schmidt!" He said with a smile.

"Yes, sir!" I replied.

"Please, have a seat," he said as he signaled towards the chair in front of the desk, in which I proceeded to sit in.

"So, you want to work the night shift?" he asked.

Five Nights At Freddy's

"Yes, sir," I replied.

"You said on the phone that you dropped out of high school and have no past work experience.

Correct?"

"Yes, that's correct."

I felt stupid talking all professional, but that's how you get the job.

"Well, the truth is, you really don't need much to work the night shift," he explained. "All you need to know how to do is look at screens and press buttons."

"Well, I play video games a lot, so I think I'm good there," I admitted.

The manager smiled.

"Now," he continued, "if you get this job, your main focus is the animatronic characters on the stage."
"Why?"

"Well, we don't want anything to happen to them; they're old and almost irreplaceable. We'd fix them, but money's kind of tight for us right now."

"Oh."

I didn't really know how to reply to that.

"Which reminds me," he then proceeded, "if you're unhappy with your payroll, I understand. Of course, perhaps your pay isn't that

Five Nights At Freddy's

important to you, or else you wouldn't have called!"

"You got me there," I said with a chuckle. "I'm mainly here because my sister forced me to. She wants me to make my parents like me again."

"I see," he said with a nod. "Well, if you're going to be watching the characters, you may as well get to know them!"
He then pointed to a picture on the wall of the three animals I had seen on stage when I entered.

"Right there in the middle is our main attraction, Freddy Fazbear," he said while pointing at the teddy bear. "Right there is Bonnie the Bunny, and that's Chica the Chicken."

"That's a chicken?" I asked in shock. "It looks like a duck!"

"Yeah, a lot of people think that," the manager said with a chuckle.

"Wait, who's that?" I asked while pointing to another picture.

The character in there was a red fox or something with an eye patch and a hook on his hand. He also had a big jaw with sharp-looking teeth.

"Oh, that's Foxy the Pirate," he replied. "He was our main attraction at Pirate Cove, but we haven't used him in years!"

"Why?"

"There was an...accident almost thirty years ago involving him," he said nervously. "It's not something we like to talk about."

"I see," I said casually.

Five Nights At Freddy's

I wonder what happened...

"Well, I think that just about covers it!" He finally said with a smile. "Still interested?"

I thought for a minute. It seemed like a simple enough job, and it would make my family happy!
"I am," I replied.

"Well, consider yourself hired!"

He then extended his hand, which I politely shook.

"You start tonight, 12 am!" He said. "Be here a bit earlier, though, so I can help you get settled."

"Sounds good!" I replied.

Well, I officially had a job now! It actually kinda felt great! Now I just got to find a way to stay awake all night.

Orientation

Five Nights At Freddy's

I arrived at the restaurant at 11:55 pm. There was only one car in the parking lot, and very few lights on in the building. I walked inside the building (the door was shockingly unlocked), and found the lights in the main stage area were the only ones on. I could still see the three characters on the stage, only they were shut off and not moving now. Somehow that made them look creepier.

I heard footsteps approaching from the back. It actually frightened me because it was so quiet before then.

The manager walked into the room to see who had come in. He smiled when he saw me.
"Welcome to your first night!" He said with glee. "Excited?"

"I guess," I replied.

"Better than a no! Follow me and I'll show you your station."

He then started heading to the back of the restaurant, and I had no choice but to follow him.
"It's pretty scary here without light, I know," he admitted, "but don't worry; you have plenty of light in your room."

"That's good to hear!" I said with relief.

He was right when he said it was scary without light. It looked nothing like the happy, joyful place I was in only hours ago.

"Here we are!"

I saw a small room with two doors, one on each side. There was definitely light in it, though, so that was good.

"There's your seat," he said, referring to the black chair in the center

Five Nights At Freddy's

of the room.

I went into the room and sat down in the chair. It was a little cramped in here, but at least I had leg and arm room.

In front of me was a desk with papers, a phone, a fan, and some food wrappers. There were posters for Freddy Fazbear's Pizza all over the walls, as well as some drawings that looked like they came from children.

Next to each of the doors were two buttons; there was a white one labeled 'LIGHT' and a red one labeled 'DOOR."

Finally, in front, was a blank screen, which I assumed was where the security feed would come from.

"Now, there's one important thing I have to tell you," the manager told me through the hallway. "Like I said, we have money problems. So we can't afford to keep the main electricity running all the time. So during your shift, the only power in the building will come from a generator that, if used properly, can last at least six hours."

"Doesn't sound too bad," I said with a shrug.

"Well, the more electrical objects are used," he explained, "the faster the battery will drain."

"Makes sense."

"Right, but you could end up using a lot of power throughout your shift. For example, the cameras use power, the door lights use power, the doors themselves use power...heck, you could just sit here and use power from the lights in the room!"

"Oh!"

Five Nights At Freddy's

I had no idea how much I would need power. I just hope it would be easy to conserve it.

"Oh, one more thing," he said.

He then pulled out a piece of paper and a pen.

"If you could sign this, that would be great."

"What is it?"

"It's basically a contract saying you'll stay here the whole time during your shift, you won't break anything, steal anything, bring a friend or relative in, you know. Legal stuff."

"Oh, ok."

So I grabbed the pen and signed it.

"Well, it's almost time for your shift to start," he said while looking at his watch. "I'm sure everything will be fine. I'll see you in the morning!"

"Alright. See you!"

I was actually really nervous; this was NOT alright. But I couldn't back out now.

He then left and I deeply exhaled. I hope this would go smoothly.

I heard a clock chime. I looked up and saw a clock that read 12:00 am. My first night had officially begun. I just hoped it would go by fast.

Night 1

Five Nights At Freddy's

I sat in the office. It was eerily quiet. The only real noise was coming from the electric fan on the desk.
I turned on the screen in front of me and was greeted with a view of the three robotic characters on the stage, only now there was no light anywhere. They looked creepier than they ever have.

To the bottom right of the screen was what looked like a layout of the building. It also appeared to be touch screen. I tapped on one of the other boxes and the screen changed to another room. This one appeared to be backstage, where lots of spare animal costumes could be found.

I caught a glimpse of a small screen to the left of the desk. It displayed a giant 99%, as well as two green bars. I turned the cameras off and suddenly there was one bar. I realize this must be my power supply reader.

Suddenly, the phone on my desk rang and I nearly jumped out of my seat. After my heart started calming again, I picked up the receiver.

"Hello?" I asked.

"*Hello?*" The voice on the other end replied.

It sounded static-y but I could tell it was a man.

"*Oh, hey! You must be the new guy.*"

"Yeah, that's me," I replied.

"*Well, I'm here to get you settled in for your first week,*" he explained. "*I used to work in that office before you. I'm actually finishing my last week now, as a matter of fact!*"

Five Nights At Freddy's

"Oh," I replied.

I really didn't know what else to say.

"So, I know it can be a bit overwhelming, but I'm here to tell you there's nothing to worry about; you'll be fine, so let's just focus on getting through your first night, okay?"

"Alright."

"Let's see...There's this introductory greeting from the company I'm suppose to read. It's kind of a legal thing, you know?"

"Of course."

*"Ok, uh...**Welcome to Freddy Fazbear's Pizza, a magical place for grown-ups and kids alike, where fantasy and fun come to life. Fazbear Entertainment is not responsible for damage to property or person.**"*

That seemed normal legal procedure.

*"**Upon discovering that damage or death has occurred, a missing persons report will be filed withing 90 days or as soon as property and premises have been thoroughly cleaned and bleached, carpets replaced,** blah blah blah."*

That did NOT seem like normal legal procedure! I thought back to what Macey said, that maybe they're just planning for the worst.

"Now, that might sound bad, I know," he continued, *"but there's really nothing to worry about!"*

Five Nights At Freddy's

I kind of wanted to believe him.

"Now, the animatronic characters here do tend to get a bit...quirky at night."

"Quirky?" I asked.

"Yeah, but do I blame them? No! If I were forced to sing those same stupid songs for twenty years and I never got a break, I'd probably get a bit irritable at night, too."

I guess he had a point.

"So remember, these characters hold a special place in the hearts of children, so we need to show them some respect. Okay?"

"Okay."

"So just be aware," he then said in a serious tone, *"these characters do tend to...wonder a bit."*

"Wander?!"

I felt like a broken record.

"Yeah, they're left in some sort of 'free roaming' mode at night. Something about their servos locking up if they're left off for too long."

"Why don't they just do that in the day time?"

"Well, they USED to be able to walk around in the day," he explained, *"but then there was 'The Bite of '87.'"*

Five Nights At Freddy's

I froze with fear. I could then hear him chuckle to himself.

"It's amazing that the human body can survive without the frontal lobe," I heard him say quietly.
I then thought of what the manager said earlier, about an 'accident occurring almost thirty years ago...Just what the hell is up with this place?!

"Now, concerning your safety," he continued in a normal tone, *"the only real risk for you as a night watchmen, if any, is that these characters...If they happen to see you after hours, probably won't recognize you as a PERSON."*

"What?" I asked. "What will they recognize me as?"

"They'll...most likely see you as a metal endoskeleton without its costume on."

That's a bit strange.

"Now, since that's against the rules here at Freddy Fazbear's Pizza, they'll probably try to...uh...forcefully stuff you inside a Freddy Fazbear suit."

That didn't seem too bad.

"Which wouldn't be so bad," he said, as if reading my mind, *"if the suits themselves weren't filled with crossbeams, wiring, and animatronic devices. Especially around the facial area."*

I suddenly cringed at the thought of that.

"So, yeah, you can probably imagine how having your face shoved in there would cause a lot of discomfort. And death."

Five Nights At Freddy's

I felt like I was about to puke.

"The only parts of you that would most likely see the light of day again would be your eyes and teeth poking out the front of the mask."

I could feel myself getting pale. I didn't make a single noise.

"Yeah, they don't tell you these things when you sign up," he replied to my silence.

"No they don't..." I replied.

"But hey, first night should be a breeze! I'll chat with you tomorrow."

"Ok..."

I was really scared.

"Remember, check those cameras and close the doors if absolutely necessary. Got to conserve power."
I looked at my power meter. It was at 98% now.

"Got it," I told him.

"Alright. Good night!"

I then heard him hang up. I then put the receiver back and deeply exhaled as I grabbed my hair. My heart was racing fast. I had no idea what this job was like.

Just out of curiosity, I turned the camera back on and turned to the stage. All three of them were there. I sighed a deep sigh of relief. I then turned the camera back off. I then just chuckled.

Five Nights At Freddy's

'He's just messing with me,' I told myself. 'He just wants to mess with the new guy. They won't move, and they certainly won't try to put me in a suit! I'll be fine.'

I then pulled out my iPod and started listening to some music while reading a magazine I brought with me.

After a while I glanced at the clock above me. It was 12:45 am. I then opened the screen again. They were all still there. I smiled and put the screen back down.

I then let out a big yawn. I tried taking a nap earlier today, but I don't think it did much help. I figured another nap wouldn't hurt. I then closed my eyes and I could feel myself passing out.

I then woke up to the sound of clanking. I suddenly opened my eyes and looked at the clock. 3:30 am. I pulled up the screen and my heart dropped; I saw a brown bear and a yellow chicken, but not a purple bunny! Bonnie was gone!

I then clicked around and when I got to the dining room area, I saw him standing by the tables.
I asked myself how he got there, but then I realized that maybe the guy on the phone was right; maybe they DO move!

Anyway, I put the camera down to not waste any power, which I saw was at 73%.

'Calm down, Mike,' I thought to myself. 'It'll be okay. He's just standing there. He's not going to get you.'

I then peeked back at the screen. He was still there and the others were still in their spots. I felt myself taking short breaths out of fear.

Five Nights At Freddy's

I put the camera back down and tried to relax. I'm sure even if those things found me, they wouldn't try to put me in one of those suits. That's just crazy!

I then heard footsteps in the hall. I quickly pulled the screen back up and saw Bonnie wasn't there. I went back to the stage and Freddy was the only one standing on the stage. My heart started pounding again.

I quickly clicked through the rooms and saw Bonnie was in the supply closet, again just standing there.

I then flicked through and found Chica by the restrooms, standing there with her mouth wide open.
After putting the camera down again, I looked at the clock. 4:33 am. Somehow time was passing by fast.

After hearing footsteps again, I turned the cameras back on again to reveal Bonnie was back in the dining room, and Chica in the kitchen. The kitchen camera was set to audio only for whatever reason, but I heard things moving in there, so I assume Chica's in there. Freddy was still there on the stage, though.

All the while, I could see my battery being used up. At 5 am it was at 44%. The manager said if used just right, this thing will last over six hours. I hoped that was true.

The characters didn't seem to be that much of a threat, to be honest. They were just moving around the building, nowhere near me. And it was only two of them. I actually felt a bit confident.

Finally, I heard chiming above me! I looked up and saw the clock that read 6 am! I sighed a deep sigh of relief. I then looked at the cameras for the heck of it, and notice Bonnie and Chica were walking back towards the stage. When they got back on it, they got back into their positions and froze.

I then pulled the screen down and got up from my chair. My first night at Freddy Fazbear's Pizza had come to an end. And I had quiet an earful for the manager!

Confrontation

I heard the front door open a few minutes after 6. I got out of my boxed room and went over to the front, where I found the manager walking in. He smiled when he saw me. I, however, didn't returned the smile.

"Thanks for watching the place!" He said.

"And thanks for telling me those robots move at night!" I told him as I pointed at them on stage.
His smile disappeared. He then sighed.

Five Nights At Freddy's

"If I would've told you that when you signed up, you would've never taken the job," he replied.

"You're right!" I replied. "But a head's up would've been considerate!"

"I'm sorry, but I had to do what I had to do."

"Well, I have to do what I have to do," I replied coldly. "I quit!"

"You can't do that!"

"Watch me!"

"No, Mr. Scmidt, you seriously cannot do that!"

"...Why?"

He then pulled out what looked like my contract out of his pocket, as if he knew he'd need it.

"Look right here," he said pointing at the paper.

I took a glance at where he was pointing and my heart stopped; it clearly read, *"As a worker, I will not quit or leave this job at all while employed at Freddy Fazbear's Pizza."*

"You son of a bitch!" I shouted.

"I'm truly sorry, but it's the only way to keep workers employed!"

"What if I don't come to work, huh?"

"Ahem...'*As a worker, if I do not work any of my shifts, I understand*

Five Nights At Freddy's

I will be sued by Fazbear Entertainment for everything I own'."

"That's just ridiculous!"

"I'm very, very sorry, Mr. Schmidt."

I then deeply sighed and stormed out of the restaurant.

"Don't forget," He called out, "your shift starts again tonight at midnight!"

I was kind enough to flip him off as I got into my car and drove off.

Five Nights At Freddy's

Night 2

I arrived to work at 11:50 pm (God forbid I get sued). The manager was in the front area again, only this time he didn't greet me with a smile. In fact, he didn't say anything at all. He just gave a quick nod and left the place. This was going to be one awkward career with him.

I then went into my office and waited until my shift officially started. Let me tell you, it was the longest ten minutes of my life.

This whole day wasn't very fun. I started sleeping as soon as I got home, and didn't get up until three in the afternoon. Macey asked how the job was. I shrugged and said it was fine. If I would've told her the truth, she would've never believed me.

Then, the clock rang 12 and I deeply exhaled as I prepared for my second night.

Five Nights At Freddy's

A minute later, the phone rang. I was sort of expecting it this time, so I wasn't surprised. The loud noise after a bit of silence will cause a scare,though.

I then picked up the phone.

"Hello?"

"Hello!"

It was the same guy from last night.

"Well hey! You made it to night two! Congrats!"

"Thanks."

"Now, I won't talk quite as long this time, seeing as how Freddy and his friends become more active as the week progresses," he explained. *"It might be a good idea to look at the cameras while I talk to make sure everyone's in their proper place."*

With that, I quickly looked at the camera and sighed with relief.

"They're still on stage," I told him.

"You know, interestingly enough, Freddy doesn't come off stage very often!"

"Really?"

That would help a lot; one less robot I have to deal with.

"Yeah, but I heard he becomes a lot more active in the dark, though...But hey, I guess that's one more reason to not out of power,

Five Nights At Freddy's

right?"

"Right," I replied with a nervous laugh.

"Oh, I also want to emphasize the importance of using your door lights," he continued.

"Good, because I was wondering what those were for."

I then pressed the white button and the hallway outside my door lit up.

"You see, there are blind spots in your camera view," he explained, *"and those blind spots happen to be right outside you doors."*

At least those were the only blind spots.

"So, you can't see something...or someone...on your camera, be sure to check your door lights. You might only have a few seconds to react...Not that would be in any danger, of course. I'm not implying that."

"Of course not."

I'm sure how unintentionally sarcastic that came out.

"Also, check on the curtain in Pirate Cove from time to time."

"Why?"

I then turned the camera on, only to discover Bonnie was off the stage. After finding him in the dining area, I switched to Pirate Cove's camera, where I just found a closed curtain with a '*Sorry, OUT OF ORDER*' sign in front.

Five Nights At Freddy's

"The character in there seems to be unique, and that he becomes more active when the cameras are turned off for a long period of time," he explained. *"I guess he doesn't like to be watched. I don't know."*

I put the camera down and thought about what he just said. The manager said the character in Pirate Cove hadn't been used in years! Why would he still be able to roam?

"Anyway, I'm sure you have everything under control," he finished. *"Talk to you soon!"*

"Alright," I told him. "Later!"

He then hung up, as did I.

I looked back at the camera and saw Bonnie was still in the dining area and everyone else was still on stage. I then flipped to Pirate Cove and saw the curtain was still closed.

This was definitely going to be an interesting shift.

An hour passed, and not much really happened. Bonnie kept moving from place to place, but thankfully he wasn't in a blind spot at all.

I kept checking in on Pirate Cove and still found the curtains shut. I don't think he was going to be a real problem.

I looked back at the stage and found Chica had moved, as well. I manage to find her by the restrooms, staring creepily.

I put the camera down and started feeling nervous. Both of them were moving now, but hey, at least Freddy hasn't moved! Although I

Five Nights At Freddy's

checked the cameras after thinking that to make sure.

Another hour passed. It was 2 am now, and not much changed. Bonnie and Chica were moving around, Freddy was still on stage, and nothing was different at Pirate Cove. Best of all, my power was at 69%, which I felt was pretty good progress.

It may have gotten a bit TOO easy, because I felt myself slowly falling asleep...

I woke up to rattling outside my left door. I quickly looked at my clock and saw it was 2:30. I flipped through the camera and checked the areas outside my left door, but I couldn't see anything.

My heart started beating fast; there was one more possibility.

I quickly pressed the white button on my left and the hallway illuminated. Instead of an empty wall, though, I was greeted by a giant purple face right in front of mine!

I shrieked in fear as I pressed the red button above the white one and I saw the giant metal door slam down.

I clutched my chest and tried to take slow, steady breaths. That thing could have easily gotten in here! I the quickly pulled the camera up again and saw Chica was still in her hallway and Freddy was still on stage.

After noticing my power was going down rapidly, I realized I couldn't keep the door shut forever. I turned on the light outside the hallway and I saw a shadow outside the window, meaning Bonnie was still there.

Maybe I DID have to leave the door shut all night...

Five Nights At Freddy's

I looked back at the the cameras and saw Chica was getting close to my door.

Freddy was still on stage though.

I turned the light back on for the left door, and saw the shadow was gone. I opened the door and saw Bonnie was no longer there. I deeply exhaled with relief and looked back at the cameras.

I then checked Pirate Cove and saw what looked like a fox head poking out between the curtains. He looked right at the camera with a widely-opened mouth and sharp teeth.

I still didn't understand why Foxy was able to roam...but that wasn't important.

I kept flipping through the cameras and found Bonnie and Chica still in the hallways, and Freddy still in place. I looked back at Pirate Cove and saw Foxy still looking at the camera. He looked pretty tore up, but I suppose that's what happens when you're abandoned for thirty years.

I put the camera down to save power and tried to calm myself. It was 3 am now and my power was at 52%. If I kept it up at this rate, I'd barely make it to 6 am.

I checked again to see where everyone was. Bonnie was in the supply closet, Freddy hadn't moved off stage, and Foxy was still peeking out the curtain; however, I couldn't find Chica. I had last seen her in the right hallway.

I then turned on the right door light and was greeted by a yellow chicken pressed against the glass window. I quickly shut the door

Five Nights At Freddy's

and turned the light off.

After a few seconds, I turned the light back on, and she was still there.

Groaning, I turned on the cameras to find everyone else. They were in their same places, but something was different about Foxy: he was farther out of the curtain! I really needed to keep an eye on him... I turned the light on again and saw Chica was gone. I then opened the door and then checked both door lights again to make sure. Nothing on either of them.

Soon, it was 5 am. Nothing else exciting really happened, save for a few times Bonnie and Chica appeared outside my doors. My power was at 31%, so I felt safe.

I then decided to check Pirate Cove again. When I did, though, I discovered the entire curtain was wide opened and Foxy was nowhere in sight! And the Out of Order sign now read **'It's Me!'**. I then quickly flipped through all my cameras to find him, only to discover he was dashing down the hallway towards my left door!

I quickly slammed the door shut when I saw him. A split second later, I heard banging on the door. Then it went completely silent. I turned the light on to make sure he was gone and I pulled the door back up.

I then checked the camera and found the curtains at Pirate Cove were closed again. I assumed that's where he was now.

After that, everything went smoothly. There was no more hiding in blind spots and there was no more Foxy attacks.

I gave a small chuckle of joy when I heard the clock ring 6 am. I then

Five Nights At Freddy's

looked and saw everyone head back to their proper places. With that, it was just a simple wait until the manager showed up. I was really starting to wonder if I could handle this job any longer than a week.

Five Nights At Freddy's

Research

"What are you doing?" Macey asked as she looked over my shoulder.

"Just doing research on Freddy Fazbear's," I replied, not taking my eyes off the computer screen.
"Why?"

"I don't know. Something just doesn't feel right about the place."

"What do you mean?"

"I...don't know."

I didn't want to lie to her, but I know how ridiculous this whole thing sounded.
"Alrighty then..." she then walked away to make us dinner.

I honestly didn't know what I'd find with my research, but I knew I had to find something that would help me or explain something.

After a quick Google search of Freddy Fazbear's Pizza, I quickly came across a shocking fact: the place was not very popular.

It has gotten poor reviews over the years and customers have not been happy with the quality.

The most recent complaint was the report of a mother who found what appeared to be blood and a mucus-like substance around the eyeballs of one of the animatronic characters. If I didn't know better, I'd be concerned, as well. Of course, I still was.

Five Nights At Freddy's

"Dinner's ready!" Macey called out.

I then closed the screen and went into the dining room.

"You okay?" She asked as I took a bite out of my Tombstone pizza.

"Yeah. Why?" I replied as I swallowed.

"I don't know. Ever since you started working, you've been acting different."

"I'm still adjusting to my new sleep schedule," I explained.

"I know...I hope that's the only reason why."

I wanted so badly to tell her that it's not the only reason, that I hated my job and I wanted out of it, and that every night has a risk of death.

"It is," I replied, and kept eating.

There wasn't much conversation after that.

Five Nights At Freddy's

Night 3

As I sat in the office to wait for my third night to start, I realized I wasn't as nervous this time. I realized I knew what was coming. I realized I had nothing much to worry about.

Five Nights At Freddy's

When I first arrived, the manager gave another quick nod and left. He must be really scared to say anything to me, not that I blame him. I may have been a little rough on him, but what he did wasn't right.

The clock rung 12. I deeply inhaled, then exhaled. I'd be fine, I knew I would be.

The phone rang again. It was to be expected at this point. I picked it up.

"Hey," I spoke into the receiver.

"*Uhh, hello?*" The Phone Guy replied. "*Hey, you're doing great! Most people don't last this long!*"

I froze with fear.

"*I mean, you know, they usually move on to other things by now,*" he quickly corrected. "*I'm not implying that they died, that's not what I meant.*"

"Of course not," I replied confidently, but then thought of that stupid contract and there was no way they could move on to 'other things'.

"*Anyway, I better not take up too much of your time,*" he continued. "*Things start getting real tonight.*"
What the hell was THAT supposed to mean?!

"*Hey, listen, I had an idea,*" he then said. "*If you happen to get caught and want to avoid getting stuffed into a Freddy suit...try playing dead! You know, go limp.*"

I was really confused as to what that meant, but then he kept explaining.

Five Nights At Freddy's

"Then there;s a chance that maybe they'll think you're an empty costume instead."
I had to admit, that was strange, but it seemed smart!

"Then again, if they think you are an empty costume, they might want to...stuff a metal skeleton into you," he then suddenly told me. *"I wonder how that would work."*

I then was freaked at the thought. There were two possible ways of putting and endoskeleton into me, and neither would feel pretty.

"Yeah, never mind, scratch that. It's best just not to get caught," he concluded.

I appreciated this guy's attempt to make me feel better, but he's not doing a good job at it.
"Uhm, ok, I'll leave you to it," he finished. *"See you on the flip side!"*

Before I could reply, he hung up. I somehow felt more nervous. What did he mean when he said things would get real tonight?!

But I had no time to figure it out. I looked at the stage through the camera, and saw Bonnie was already off stage. After finding him backstage, I then checked om Pirate Cove and found the curtains closed. So far, everything seemed alright.

Time seemed to pass quickly as I kept flipping through the cameras, keeping an eye on everyone. Bonnie and Chica were both moving now, Foxy's head was sticking out of the curtain, and Freddy was suddenly staring at me on stage. It was the first time Freddy showed any signs of movement ever since I started working.

By the time it was 3 am, my power had dropped to 48%. As long as I

Five Nights At Freddy's

used little power as possible, I'll be fine.

I kept checking my blind spots often to make sure nobody was nearby and ready to kill me. I didn't fully believe they'd do much harm to me, but I couldn't risk it.

Finally, at 4 am, I checked Pirate Cove and discovered the curtain was wide open and Foxy was nowhere to be found. I immediately shut the left door again and pulled up my screen. I checked the hallway outside the door and found Foxy sprinting down the hallway again. When he got outside my door, he banged on it a few times before stopping and leaving.

I deeply exhaled and opened the door again. Suddenly, I heard a deep and creepy laugh echo throughout the building. I then pulled up the scree and my heart started pounding; Freddy wasn't on the stage.

I checked the dining area and at first I didn't see anything, but a close look at the screen revealed two small white lights in a dark corner of the room. I then remembered the Phone Guy telling me Freddy becomes a lot more active in the dark.

I then kept checking where everyone was. Foxy was still behind the curtain, Bonnie was in the supply closet, Chica was in the right hallway, and Freddy was still in the dining area.

Soon, it was 5 am. Freddy was still in the dining area, Foxy was barely peeking out of the curtain, and Bonnie and Chica were still wandering around. Occasionally, I had to shut the doors, but my power was alright.

However, I took a glance at the remaining power and saw it was 14%. I wasn't sure if I'd have enough to make it.

Five Nights At Freddy's

Suddenly, I heard the deep, creepy laugh again. I opened the screen and saw Freddy was no longer in the dining area. I flipped through and found him in the restrooms with, again, white lights in a dark area.

Soon, I looked at my power supply. It was at 3% and it was 5:56 am. A miracle from God himself would let me make it.

I checked the screens again and saw everyone hadn't moved, which was good.

Finally, my power was at 1%. It was 5:59 am. I felt confident, yet scared. I decided to stop using the camera and lights. It was risky, but it was worth it.

Finally, the clock rang 6! I opened the camera with the last of my shift's power, and saw everyone go back to their place. I then realized that if nothing else changed at this point, I would be ok.

I still felt like some things about this place were a bit off. I'd need to do more research about the place to find out more.

Five Nights At Freddy's

Night Shift 101

When the manager showed up, I left without saying a word, as did he. As I left and headed for my car, though, I someone give a quick whistle for attention. I looked around and saw what looked like a homeless man in the alleyway a few buildings over.

"Hey, you!" He called out. "You that new security guard over at there pizza place?"

"Um...Yes," I replied slowly.

"Come here!" He called out to me. "I can help you!"

Did he somehow know about what happens in the place?

"Um...I'm actually kind of tired," I told him. Which wasn't a lie.

"Do you want to die tomorrow?"

Five Nights At Freddy's

"No..."

"Then get over here so I can help you!"

I paused before exhaling and jogging towards him. If I was going to potentially die, I'd rather it be from a hobo than a robot.

"Listen," he said quietly when I got to him. "Your next shift will be your fourth night, right?"

"Yeah," I replied.

"And has that evil bear ever started moving yet?"

"Yeah!"

"Let me tell you, he's a sneaky one! You'll never see him get in your room until it's too late!"

"What do you mean?!"

"I mean, you got to keep your eyes on him at all times! When you look in your cameras and don't see him, he's already in there with you!"

"I'm sorry, but how do you know all this?"

"I used to work at that goddamned place myself," he replied.

"But, how did you quit?"

"Quit?!"

He then burst into laughter.

Five Nights At Freddy's

"Boy, I didn't quit! I couldn't!"

"So...What happened?"

"I didn't show up for work, that's what!"

"So...That means you..."

"...Got sued for everything I own? Yes, I did. That's why I am how I am now."

"I'm so sorry..."

"Hey, it was the best experience of my life! After that, I got fired and I was free from that hell!"
"So, why are you here?"

"To warn guards to come about how to survive that job!"

"Well, if all I have to do is watch for Freddy..."

He then laughed again.

"You think that's all?! You also got to watch for the bunny and ducky-thing!"

"Why?"

"Those bastards can break your wiring! If you don't lock them out in time, they'll stop your lights and door from functioning properly! Then they'll get you as soon as you put down that monitor."

"How do you know?"

Five Nights At Freddy's

"I've seen it happen to innocent fools who didn't know better..."

"So what do I do if that happens?"

"The only thing you can do is close the other door and just sit there. No using the camera or any electronic of the sort. You got to conserve what power you have left!"

"That's risky..."

"But it's the only way!"

I didn't know how to reply. I was wondering how serious this guy was. Maybe the job made him too crazy.

"Well...Thanks for the advice."

"Remember what I said!" He said sternly.

"I will," I replied.

I then went back towards my car.

"Remember: watch the bear and keep that bunny and duck from breaking the wires!"

"Got it!"

I then got in my car and pulled away. I began thinking of what he said. I had a feeling I REALLY wasn't going to like my fourth night.

Five Nights At Freddy's

Macey's Research

"Mike, can I talk to you?" Macey asked.

"Sure, I guess," I replied and muted the TV.

"You know how you said something about that pizza place you work at didn't feel right?"

"Yeah...?"

"Well, while you were sleeping this morning, I did my own research

Five Nights At Freddy's

on the place,"

"Did you find something?"

I was actually curious.

"Unfortunately, yes."

"Unfortunately?"

She then handed me some news articles that she had cut out from the newspaper.

The first one read **"Kids Vanish at Local Pizzeria-Bodies Not Found"**

That immediately got my attention. I kept reading.

"Two local children were reportedly lured into a back room during the late hours of operation at Freddy Fazbear's Pizza on the night of June 26th. While video surveillance identified the man responsible and led to his capture the following morning, the children themselves were never found and are presumed dead. Police think that the suspect dressed as a mascot to earn the children's trust."

"Holy shit..." I said quietly.

"It gets worse," she explained. "Read the next one."

So I pulled the next article out and read it.

"Five children now reported missing-suspect convicted."

Five Nights At Freddy's

"Five children are now linked to the incident at Freddy Fazbear's Pizza, where a man dressed as a cartoon mascot lured them into a back room. While the suspect has been charged, the bodies themselves were never found. Freddy Fazbear's Pizza has been fighting an uphill battle ever since to convince families to return to the pizzeria."

"That's strange...When I went for the interview, everything seemed fine! There were kids all over the place, happy as can be!"

"Keep going," she commanded. She was really starting to look nervous.

I looked at the last article she had given me.

"Local Pizzeria threatened with shutdown over sanitation."

"Local pizzeria Freddy Fazbear's Pizza has been threatened again with shutdown by the health department over reports of foul odor coming from the much-loved animal mascots. Police were contacted when parents reportedly noticed what appeared to be blood and mucus around the eyes and mouths of the mascots. One parent called them "reanimated carcasses'."

I read about this one a little bit last night," I admitted.

"Mike...What the fuck is going on here?!"

I sighed. I could tell how worried she was about this. So I told her everything. I told her about the Phone Guy's messages, I told her about my contract that prevents me from leaving. I told her about the homeless man's advice. I told her about the possibility of dying by being shoved into a costume. By the time I was done explaining, she looked sickly pale.

Five Nights At Freddy's

"Why didn't you tell me this before?" She finally asked.

"Would you have believed me?"

She replied with silence.

"If I would've told you that on my first night back, you would've said I was overreacting about work and I that I was trying to get out of it."

More silence. It looked like she was about to tear up.

"Can't you just call the police or something?" She asked after a while.

I shook my head.

"I caught a glimpse of the contract. It read *"If, at any time, I call the police while employed at Freddy Fazbear's Pizza, I understand I will be sued for everything I own."*

"That's ridiculous!" Macey said with a reddened face.

I just shrugged.

"Not much I can do," I replied.

"Well, all I can say is...Go to work tonight and try to survive. Take the homeless man's advice and keep and eye on everyone. I'll try to do more research, maybe find a way around your contract."

"You'd do that?" I asked.

Five Nights At Freddy's

"Of course, Mike! You're my brother and I love you! I got to make sure you're okay at all times."

"Thanks, Macey...Really."

She then smiled and looked at her watch. The smile quickly faded.

"It's about time for you to leave," she told me.

I gave a quick nod and got ready. Before I left, she gave me a tight hug and started crying.

"It's all my fault..." She whispered. "I HAD to make you take this stupid job."

"It's okay," I replied while patting her back. "There's no way you would've known."

"I know..."

"I'll be fine," I told her confidently. "Honest."

"Alright, be safe."

With that, I said bye and left for work. I was starting to wonder what happened to those kids that went missing. When I got into my car, though, it hit me; maybe, just maybe, those missing children are inside the animatronic suits. It would make sense; that's why the bodies were never found and it's why the characters had a foul odor, and had blood and mucus around the eyes and mouth. But there were only four characters...And five kids. I wonder where the fifth one went?

As I pulled out of the driveway, I asked myself if I could keep my promise to Macey.

Night 4

I couldn't stop thinking about the articles Macey showed me. If I was correct, and the children were in the suits, it would explain so much. Of course, it raised the possibility of...a haunting.
I was never one to believe in ghosts or the supernatural, but after this whole job, I realized anything is possible. It may be possible that those kids are possessing the costumes, which is why they move around. I know the Phone Guy claimed there was a 'free-roaming' mode, but I began wondering if that was the whole reason they walk around.

Before I could reflect more on it, the clock rang 12. I pulled up the camera and found everyone in their place.

When the phone rang, I didn't flinch at all. I just picked up the phone with confidence.
"Hello?" I asked.

"*Hello, hello?*" It was him again. "*Hey! Her, wow, day four. I knew you could do it.*"
He somehow seemed nervous.

"*Uh, hey, listen, I may not be around to send you a message tomorrow.*" I could suddenly hear banging in the background. "*It's-*

Five Nights At Freddy's

it's been a bad night here for me. Uhm, I'm kind of glad that I recorded this message for you when I did."

I had a terrible feeling this wasn't going to end well. Wait...This was a recording?!

"Hey, do me a favor," he continued as the banging increased. *"Maybe sometime, you could check inside one of those suits in the backroom? I'm gonna try to hold out until someone checks. Maybe it won't be so bad."* The banging wouldn't stop. *"Uhh...I always wondered what was in those empty heads back there..."*

I then suddenly heard what sounded like a music box playing a song that sounded very creepy.
"You know..."

There was then what sounded like a low pitched moaning, similar to what I've heard Bonnie and Chica make.

"Oh, no...!"

There was suddenly a loud-pitched screeching sound echoing through the phone, then the phone disconnected.

I sat in fear. I wanted to believe he was okay, but I somehow knew that wasn't very likely.
I then opened the screen to reveal Bonnie and Chica were gone. After finding them in the cameras, I checked Pirate Cove, only to discover Foxy was already sticking out between the curtains. This was going to be a fun night.

For the first hour, I managed to find Bonnie and Chica scattered all over the place, but thankfully they weren't in a blind spot. Foxy was still teasing me by sticking out from the curtains, staring at me.

Five Nights At Freddy's

Freddy, however, remained still on the stage.

I began to feel confident now. I felt like there was nothing to worry about.

I checked the light outside my doors. The right one was clear. The left, however, was filled with a purple bunny! I then slammed the door shut and checked the cameras again. Chica was by the restrooms, Foxy was sticking out of the curtains, and Freddy...Oh shit...I couldn't find Freddy!
I heard that same evil, low-pitched laugh echo through the building again.

I checked to see if Bonnie was outside the door. Thankfully he wasn't. I opened the door and looked at the camera.

In the dining area, I could see the two glowing eyes in the dark again. The homeless guy said I just had to keep my eye on him and I'd be fine.

I checked Pirate Cove again and found the curtain wide open. I quickly shut the left door. A second later, there was banging on the door. I then froze. That sounded like the banging I had heard in the phone call.

Anyway, I checked the light and there was nobody in the hallway. I opened the door with relief. I then suddenly heard the evil laugh again.

I opened the camera and tried to find Freddy. I didn't see any glowing lights anywhere, but when I checked the kitchen's camera, despite it being audio only, I heard the familiar music box playing the similar song that was playing in the phone call. I could only

Five Nights At Freddy's

assume Freddy was in the kitchen. I managed to find everyone else, so I was safe for now.

I then flipped through the cameras and in one hallway, I found something I hadn't seen before: a poster of what looked like Freddy, but he seemed to be golden, despite the black and white feed of the camera.
I was confused, but I shrugged and put the screen down. When I did, I saw what appeared to be the same Freddy I just saw on the poster sitting right in front of me. It was golden, limping lifelessly, and had empty eye sockets and no teeth at all.

Screaming, I pulled the screen back up to protect myself from it. I then flipped through the cameras again to find everyone. Surprisingly, I did it to calm myself down.

When I found them all in the same places, I dared myself to put the camera down. I was relieved when I saw that the Golden Freddy was gone. I wondered if that was really there, or if I was imagining it. Anyway, I soon looked at the clock. 5:55 am. I could make this. I could! I then looked at my power and my heart dropped. I was at 1%. There was no way to make it now. Without power, I had no way of protecting myself.

Suddenly, the light in my room shut off, the camera screen stopped working, and a loud humming slowly went low-pitched as the power went out. I was now sitting in total darkness.

I sat completely still in my seat. Maybe I could still make it. I only had to wait five more minutes.
For the next four minutes, I sat in complete silence. I didn't move at all, and I made no noises. I could hear the characters moving around in the building, which made my heart race.

Five Nights At Freddy's

Suddenly, I heard that music box song playing, only it sounded extremely close. I felt sweat roll down my face. I remembered my promise to Macey, that I'd be okay tonight. I felt terrible that I couldn't keep that promise.

Suddenly, the music stopped. I could hear footsteps slowly approaching. I held my breath. This is it. I was going to die.

Then I heard it; the clock! It was battery operated! It rang 6 am! I heard the footsteps quickly fading as I sat in my room trying to catch my breath. I barely survived night four. I was terrified for what tomorrow would bring, and if I would survive it.

Five Nights At Freddy's

Discovery

I knew I had a few minutes before the manager would show up, so I decided to do something real quick. I silently stepped out of the office and ran towards the back room, where all the animal costumes were.

I see the live feed of this room every night, but I've never seen it in person. It looked the same, but felt very uneasy. One reason for that was the horrible smell.

I felt like I was going to gag as I walked in, it was just so foul-smelling. I then looked at the corner of the room with the security camera. I had seen something I hadn't seen in the feed: a Freddy suit that appeared to be a spare! It was slouched over and lifeless, and had no signs of a metal endoskeleton.
I also managed to figure out that it was the source of the foul smell! I wondered what was going on with it, but I knew the Phone Guy wanted me to see this. I realized that he wanted me to check, because there might be something horrible inside.

I heard the front door open up.

"Mr. Schmidt?" The manager called out. "Where are you?"

"In the back room," I replied.

I could hear total silence.

"Why?" He finally asked.

Five Nights At Freddy's

"I smelled something in here," I told him. "I wanted to see what it was."

"So, you left the office during your shift?"

"No! I just got in here, I promise. Check the camera yourself."

He then poked his head in the doorway.

"I'll be sure to," he promised.

"You might want to wash these suits," I told him, playing dumb. "They smell like someone died in them."

He just stared at me blankly.

"Of course," he finally said. "I'll make sure it's done."

With that, I walked out and left. I needed all the rest I could for tonight.

Confusing Truth

"Mike! You aren't going to believe this!" Macey exclaimed as I walked in the door.

She had rings around her eyes. How late did she stay up? Did she even sleep?

"What is it?" I asked.

She gave me another printout of another newspaper article. I took a look at it.

"It was printed a month after the last one I showed you," she

Five Nights At Freddy's

explained.

I then read the story:

"Local Pizzeria said to close by year's end."

"After a long struggle to stay in business after the tragedy that struck there many years ago, Freddy Fazbear's Pizza has announced that it was close by year's end. Despite a year-long search for a buyer, companies seem unwillingly to be associated with the company."
"These characters will live on in the hearts of children."
-CEO

I just stared at the article and looked up at Macey.

"I'll be damned!" I said with a chuckle. "I guess that's one prayer answered!"

"No, Mike...You clearly didn't read everything."

"What do you mean?"

"Look at the date."

I then looked at the date on the article.

"I see it. It says August 15...1997?!"

"I checked all the articles. They were all from that year."

"That doesn't make sense! I mean...shouldn't it be closed by now?"

"I don't know, Mike. But I'm worried. Something's definitely not right here."

I then thought about this for a second. If this place was supposed to be closed seventeen years ago for sanitation and business problems, how has nobody noticed that it's still opened?

"Mike, we need to call someone."

"Who? The cops? And tell them what?"

"That Freddy Fazbear's Pizza is still open! That's got to break some sort of code."

"They'd never believe us," I replied. "It would just be better to fix this ourselves."

"How?!"

"I honestly don't know yet. But I'm sure I'll have something in mind tonight."

"Tonight?"

"I still have a job you know. A job that I can't leave unless I want to be sued."

"Forget about being sued! This is more important!"

"Macey, don't worry. I have an idea."

I then explained everything I was thinking. She looked sickened, but then confused.

"Are you sure?" She asked.

Five Nights At Freddy's

"Yes," I replied. "I'm sure."

She then looked like she was going to cry again. I hugged her tightly.

"Let's just get some sleep," I told her. "We cold both use it.

She quietly agreed and went into her bedroom, and I went into mine. I had no idea if I was right, but it would be worth is if it was.

Night 5

I sat in my office, confused as ever. When I first arrived, the manager stated he made sure the suits were cleaned. I thanked him. That's when I asked him.

"Excuse me," I told him, "what's the date?"

"Hmm?"

He seemed confused.

Five Nights At Freddy's

"What's today's date? I forgot."

"Well, it's September 16th, 1997."

I stared at him. I knew he'd say that. I then nodded my head and thanked him. He then left for the night.
I am now fully convinced that this place is haunted somehow. I've heard stories of spirits being trapped in buildings and reliving the same life from their time over and over. This must be one of those cases.
Now I'm sitting in the office, waiting for my fifth night at Freddy's to start.

Suddenly, my phone rang. It wasn't my work phone, though; it was my cell phone.

I pulled it out of my right pocket and saw it was Macey. I answered.

"Hello?" I asked.

"Mike!" She replied. "I...I'm so scared."

"It'll be fine," I told her.

"What if it's not, Mike? Huh?"

I wasn't sure how to answer that.

"Don't worry about me. I there's trouble, I'll call you."

"Immediately?"

"Immediately."

Five Nights At Freddy's

"Okay...I love you, Mike."

I couldn't remember the last time I heard her say that to me.

"I love you, too, Macey."

Suddenly, the clock rang 12.

"I got to go Macey. I'll talk to you soon."

"Ok...bye."

I then hung up and opened the screen. Everyone was in their proper place. That was good. It's just what I needed.

Then, the phone rang. I was actually surprised. I thought the Phone Guy hadn't made it. I picked up the phone.

"Hello?"

What happened next would haunt me forever; some strange, creepy, almost demonic sounds could be heard being played through the phone. It was really deep and haunting, almost as if it was slowed down and backwards. It continued playing for about thirty seconds before a loud screeching blared through the phone and it hung up.

I then placed the phone back and opened the screen. Bonnie was gone. What a surprise. I found him in the back room. The room with the smelly Freddy suit.

I then checked Pirate Cove. Foxy wasn't out of his curtain yet. Good, at least that's something positive.
As the night passed, I began to wonder if I'd make it through the night. I mean, right now it was 1:03 am, and my power was at 86%. I

Five Nights At Freddy's

guess that was good, but Bonnie and Chica were wondering about. It wasn't too bad, but Foxy was starting to peek out of the curtain a bit. Thankfully, Freddy hasn't moved.

I managed to lose sight of Chica at one point. I checked the kitchen and didn't hear any sounds. I quickly turned on the light on the right hallway. Sure enough, that freaking chicken was against the window. I slammed the door shut and opened the camera. Foxy was almost out of his curtain, and Freddy was staring at me on stage with creepy eyes. However, I couldn't find Bonnie.

I turned on the left hallway light and found that damn purple bunny. I closed that door as well.

I then realized this was the first time I'd shut both doors at the same time. I looked at my power and saw it decreasing rapidly. I checked both lights and saw Chica and Bonnie are still there. To make matters worse, I heard Freddy's laugh start to echo again. I opened the camera and found him hiding in the bathrooms. Foxy was the least difficult to handle right now. I knew how dangerous this could all end.

I put the camera down and checked the hallway lights again. Chica was still there, but fortunately, Bonnie moved. I opened that door and checked the camera again. Freddy was still in the bathroom, Bonnie was in the hallway,and Foxy was already sprinting down the hallway.

I slammed the door instantly and heard banging. I waited a few seconds, turned on the light, confirmed he wasn't there, and opened the door. I checked the right light, and Chica was gone. I sighed with relief as I opened the door. I then heard Freddy's laugh again.

I opened the cameras and found him hiding in an unimaginably dark hallway near my door! He wasn't close enough to possibly enter, but he was still close. I really needed to keep my eye on him.

I looked at the time and the power. It was 2:54 am, and my power

Five Nights At Freddy's

was at 43%. It would take miracle to survive now.

I kept having frequent hallway visits from bonnie and Chica, as well as Foxy, but my main focus was keeping my eyes on Freddy. He was still in the hallway. I wanted it to stay that way.
Finally, at 5:09 am. I looked at my power. 2%. I couldn't conserve it well enough. I actually started crying. There was no way I was going to make it. There's no way they'd go a little less than an hour without finding me!

With that, I made the ultimate decision.

I shut both of my doors. I then pulled out my cell phone and called Macey. Her phone rang for what seemed like forever. Finally, I heard her voice.

"Hi, you've reached Macey Schmidt! I'm sorry I can't answer the phone right now. Leave a message and I'll get back to you as soon as I can! Thanks!"

I couldn't believe it. It was her freaking voice mail. I heard the beep, signaling my cue to leave a message. I sighed as tears rolled down my face. I was scared. I really was.

"Macey..." I started the message. "I...I'm in trouble. It's not even close to six am and my power's about to run out. If, by some miracle, I make it, that's fine. But if I don't make it...Just know that I love you. And I want to thank you for everything. Thank you for letting me stay with you, and thank you for not giving up on me. Tell Mom and Dad that I love them, too. Tell them I'm sorry for disappointing the,. But that I didn't go has a coward."

I didn't plan on doing that.

Five Nights At Freddy's

"And one more thing," I concluded. "Make sure that, no matter what happens, this place gets it! Do whatever it takes for Freddy Fazbear's Pizza to get hell!"

And that's when it happened. As soon as I said that, the lights went off and the doors opened. I paused. This was it. My last chance to say my last thoughts to her.

"Goodbye, Macey," I finally said. "Again, thank you for caring about me. I love you. And just remember that none of this was your fault."

I lost it. I dropped my phone and sobbed like a little baby. I knew full well I was going to die right now. I just knew it.

After I managed to control myself a bit, I picked up the phone and hung up. As much as I didn't want her last image of me to be crying my eyes out, I couldn't think of anything else to say.

I sat in total silence. I didn't say a word. I didn't move a muscle. I couldn't see the clock because it was so dark, but I can imagine I was sitting for only five minutes.

That's when I heard it. That damn music. The one that played last night, just as Freddy was approaching my room. It was unimaginably close. I held my breath.

This was it. I was going to die. They would get me and stuff me into a suit, just like the Phone Guy. I felt so stupid for thinking I'd survive a week at a place like this.

Then, the music stopped. There was total silence for a few seconds before I heard footsteps near the left door. I couldn't tell if they were going away...or towards me.

Five Nights At Freddy's

I sat still for what seemed like an hour. Did they leave? Are they gone? Did they think I wasn't there? Was I actually going to make it?!

AIIIIIIIIEEEEEEE!!!!!

I heard that loud screeching sound I heard on the phone right I my ears as Freddy appeared right in my face! I screamed in panic and surprise, but not for long; Freddy then grabbed my arm and yanked me out of the office.

I was now being dragged on the floor with the robot's tight grib on my left arm. I could make out some posters in the hallway as I flew by them pretty fast.

All the while, I was screaming as loud as I could in both pain and fear. I didn't know if anyone could hear me, but it was worth a shot.

However, nobody showed up as I found myself in the back room. I could see an empty Freddy Fazbear suit sitting there, already in position. Like they knew they were going to get me tonight.

I then gathered my strength, reach up towards my attacker, and hit him in the head. It seemed to do the trick, as he quickly let go of me and grabbed where I had hit him. I proceeded to get up and bolt towards the door. Contract or no contract, I was getting the hell out of here.

Escape?

Five Nights At Freddy's

I bolted out of the back room with all my stamina. I knew the exit was really close; just a turn and a sprint would do it.

I ran through the backstage area and onto the stage, where I saw the exit in plain sight. However, I could also see the silhouette of a bunny right in front of it!

I knew I couldn't risk going over there without him getting me. I had to either wait it out, or find another escape. Seeing as how I have four of these guys after me and no light to see them approach, I had to stay in motion and find another way out.

I quietly headed towards the opposite direction of Bonnie and quickly found myself in front of what appeared to be Pirate Cove. The main giveaway was Foxy peeking out between the curtains, slowly looking around. I could see him stare at the camera, which obviously wasn't working now.
I wondered if these guys had night vision, or they fully relied on sounds. I wanted to know for sure, but I needed to figure it out safely.

I saw a drinking straw on the floor. The janitor clearly needs to be fired. Of course, he might have the same contract as me.

Anyway, I picked up the straw and carefully waved it in front of Foxy's face. He didn't seem to be bothered by it at all! He just continued to stare at the turned-off camera.

I then carefully placed the straw back down on the floor and, as quietly as I could, sneaked around Foxy. I wanted to give off a sigh of relief, but I remembered how absolutely quiet I had to be.

I then kept walking down the left hallway. Shockingly, this was the first time I've actually been down this part of the restaurant. I usually

Five Nights At Freddy's

go down the right hallway to get to the office.

I found nothing but doors, including the empty and open one of my office. As much as I'd love to hide in there for protection, I had nothing to protect myself with! I just had to keep moving.

I realized, though, cutting through the office would take me to the other hallway. I decided to do just that and go back towards the exit. Maybe Bonnie would have moved by then!

I then went down the right hallway very quietly. As I passed the restrooms, I could hear that deep, evil laugh. I moved along faster, but just as quietly.

As I came closer to the dining area, I heard some clanking to my right. I looked and saw it was the entrance to the kitchen! I paused. I knew there was a character in there, but I never did get to see what was inside the kitchen.

I slowly crept towards the door and took a peek inside. It was really dark, but I could see a yellow figure just a few feet in front of me. It was walking around, bumping into the counters and stuff.
It then quickly started turning around. I quickly but quietly ran away and went towards the dining area. I really hope Chica didn't see me.

After making it safely through the dining area, I found myself in the stage area again. It was still fairly dark, but I didn't see any signs of Bonnie or any other animatronic.

I was so happy, I was so close to escape. I then quickly tiptoed towards the door. It felt like entering the gates to heaven, only without dying.

I stopped just as I got to the door. I turned around and took one last

Five Nights At Freddy's

look at Freddy Fazbear's Pizza.

"Goodbye, you hellhole!" I whispered quietly. "It was nice knowing-"

AIIIIIIIIEEEEEEEE!!!!!

Bonnie jumped right in front of me and screeched the same screech as Freddy. He then grabbed me by the arm and yanked me towards the back room.

I couldn't believe it. I was so close to freedom and I blew by wishing this place goodbye. I felt like an idiot.

I tried hitting Bonnie in the head, like I did with Freddy, but this time I was grabbed by my right arm, and my left arm was still in pain from when Freddy grabbed it.

It was no use. Nothing can save me now.

Five Nights At Freddy's

The Final Showdown

I saw the spare Freddy suit that seemed specially prepared for me still in the room. Bonnie didn't have as tight of a grip on me as Freddy did, so that could prove to be an advantage.

He then reached for my other arm. Now was my chance. I wiggled my trapped arm around furiously to get it loose. However, Bonnie suddenly seemed to get a tighter grip on me. He then yanked my arm towards the suit. I used my free hand to grab my trapped arm and pull back.

That's when it happened. Bonnie bent my right arm. Not at the elbow, but at the bone itself. I screamed in absolute pain as I heard the sharp **SNAP** echo through the room.

After that, I lost focus on my other hand and dropped it. Bonnie then rammed my broken arm into the suit's right arm.

I realized I'd be dead if I didn't do something. Without thinking, I reached behind and punched Bonnie in the face. I must have hit him harder than I thought, because the next think I knew, I heard a loud THUNK. I turned around and saw what looked like a mask lying on the ground. I then looked up at Bonnie.

Instead of his creepy, purple bunny face, it was now a child's head smashed into a metal face. The child was a little boy, maybe around six years old. He was bloody and disgusting and smelled horrible. But this confirmed my biggest suspicion of what happened to those kids all those years ago.

Five Nights At Freddy's

Just then, a quick flash of light came from the human head and Bonnie collapsed. He then stopped moving. I think he was officially gone for good.

I tried to get my arm out, but it appeared to be stuck. I could feel a sharp pain all throughout my arm, but I couldn't tell if it was because it had a shattered bone or if there were so many metal objects inside. Either way, it hurt so much when I tried to pull on it.

I then heard a noise behind me. I turned around and didn't see anyone, or anything, moving. I was really confused and just hoped it was my imagination. But that hoped turned into doubt real fast.

AIIIIIIIEEEEEEEE!!!!!!

Chica appeared and tackled me to the ground, pulling my arm causing me to cry in pain. The chicken then grabbed my left leg and tried stuffing it into the suit. I used both of my legs to try and fight it off, but it was no use.

SNAP!

I could feel my leg shatter as I howled in pain. I barely had enough nerves left to feel my broken leg being stuffed into the suit.

I then punched Chica hard in the face, and her mask came off as well. I just suspected, inside the robot was a metal endoskeleton...and a dismantled head of a child. This time, however, it was a little girl, maybe about eight years old. I almost vomited at the smell. Then, just like Bonnie, a light flashed from the girl's head and the robot body collapsed. It then stopped moving. Permanently.

Now my right arm and left leg were broken and stuck in this suit. It would take a professional help to get me out.

Five Nights At Freddy's

I then heard a fast-paced sprinting near the room. I stood still in fear.
There was only one character I've seen sprint...

AIIIIIIIIEEEEEEE!!!!!

Foxy barged through the door and ran at me with his hooked arm
above his head. I tried punching his face, but he ducked out of the
way just in time. He then quickly thrust his hook into my arm.

I kept crying in pain as more of my limbs got destroyed. Foxy then
took my hooked, only remaining, arm and shoved that into the suit,
as well.

Using what will power I had left, I used my leg to reach up and kick
Foxy right in the jaw. His entire face flew across the room and
crashed into a few spare masks.

Again, there was a child's face inside the robot's head. A little boy
who's face was so mangled that I couldn't even tell how old he was.

A light appeared inside the robotic skull and the pirate fell. I was
glad about that one; I never liked Foxy.

That just left only one possessed character remaining...

Right on cue, the deep, creepy laugh echoed. It sounded
unimaginably close. I didn't care, though. This time, I was ready for
Freddy.

AIIIIIIIIEEEEEEE!!!!!

He then lunged towards me in a leap. I kicked him right in the center
of the face, in his big black nose. I heard a horn honking as I did it.

Five Nights At Freddy's

He then flew backwards and crashed into the other suits. He stood still for the longest time.

I slowly limped my way over to Freddy. It hurt so much, but I didn't care. I had to do this.

I looked over Freddy. His face was practically collapsed on itself, thanks to me. I then kicked off the mask. There was a little girl's face inside. My best guess on age was ten.

I still couldn't believe it. All this time, the robots were possessed by the missing children and nobody knew.

Then a light flashed from the girl's head. Only this time, it was super bright and lasted for about five seconds.

I don't know whether it was because of the light or pain, but the next thing I knew, I was collapsing, myself, and passed out.

Five Nights At Freddy's

Rescue

I heard the clock chiming. I wasn't sure if it was in my dreams or not. I slowly opened my eyes and looked around. At first, I had forgotten what happened. Then I felt sharp pains all over my limbs, and I remembered.

I tried sitting up with all my strength. It took time, but I managed to get up and look around the room. It somehow looked worse than it did before. There was dust and cobwebs all over the walls and corners, and the spare animal suits were ripped to shreds.

I then dared to look at the floor. When I did, I saw the four animatronic characters I had destroyed laying down, exactly how

Five Nights At Freddy's

they were when I passed out. Only this time, I noticed something different: the children were gone. All I could see inside the heads were the animatronic skeletons.

I then smiled. I had done it. I freed the children trapped here for almost twenty years. And now that they were gone, there would be no more problems with this place.

I then looked down next to Freddy and saw a yellow piece of rectangular paper, as well as a pink square, I hadn't seen earlier. I limped over to it and took a look at it. I scoffed when I saw what it was.

"Good job, Sport!" Was all the pink Post-It read. Next to it was a yellow check for one-hundred and twenty dollars in my name. It was a week's pay. I then started laughing uncontrollably. I really could care less about the money at this point.

I stopped laughing when my arms and legs started hurting. I then noticed I was still half-out of the Freddy suit. I was definitely stuck in this thing good.

Suddenly, I heard the front doors open. I sat still. It wasn't the manager, was it?

"Mike!"

I sighed with relief. It wasn't the manager, it was...

"Macey!"

"Where are you? Are you okay?"

"I'm in the back room! And I think I definitely need to go to the hospital!"

Five Nights At Freddy's

I heard footsteps rapidly approach the door before I saw my sister rush into the room. When she did, she stopped dead in her tracks and looked around at everything. At the filthiness, at the broken robots, at her brother inside a costume.

"What happened?" She finally asked quietly.

"I'll tell you later," I said, wincing in pain. "Get me to the hospital! My arms and leg are broken."
"Oh, shit!" She gasped. "Ok, hang on."

She then rushed over to me and carefully picked me up. I winced in pain, but I had to suck it up.
It's a good thing she was stronger than she looked; picking up my weight, as well as the weight of this suit, couldn't have been easy.

It took maneuvering, but she managed to get a tight grip on me and carried me out of the back room.
"I couldn't believe you worked in a dump like this," she said.

"It's not that bad," I argued.

"Mike, it's like this place hasn't been used in decades!"

"...What?"

We then got on stage and I got a good view of the whole area. I gasped when I did. Macey was right; it was like this place was abandoned for years!

Everything was covered in dust, the tables were flipped, and windows were boarded up. I kind of wanted to see the rest of the building, but I also wanted to get as far from here as possible!

Five Nights At Freddy's

"Let's just go," she told me.

"Let's!" I told her.

We then went to the door and left the restaurant. I managed to get one last look at it. I smiled when I did. This place has caused enough pain for a lifetime. I was glad to finally get away.

Epilogue

"Need anything, Mike?" Macey asked as she popped her head into my bedroom.

"Actually," I replied from my bed, "I could use some food."

She smiled.

"I'll make some pizza."

Five Nights At Freddy's

I then got a scared look on my face.

"Um...Could I have ramen noodles instead?"
"Sure!"

She then left to prepare my meal. After all that's happened, the last think I want to have on my mind is pizza.

It had been about a month since my fifth, and last, night at Freddy Fazbear's Pizza. The doctors had to cut the Freddy suit off of me and then spent hours fixing my arms and leg. The medication they prescribed helped, but it still didn't get rid of the pain altogether.

The doctor said it would take time, but my limbs would eventually heal. He also said I wouldn't be ale to go to work during the healing process. He looked so confused when I started laughing like a maniac.
Anyway, I am now confined to my bed with my arms and left leg in casts and suspended in the air. It wasn't the comfiest setup, but I didn't complain. I don't think I'll ever complain again.

Macey noew checks on me constantly, seeing if I need food or anything. I'm really glad I called her when the power went out; that message was why she came that morning.

She told me the other day that Freddy Fazbear's was now set to be torn down soon. It was the happiest news I had ever received.

Macey finally brought and fed me my noodles. We talked a bit about thus and that. Mom and Dad are concerned, of course, but they seemed to calm down when I said it was a work injury. I don't think they'll mind me not working for a long time.

Five Nights At Freddy's

Finally, it was time for bed. Macey and I said our goodnights and she went to bed. I then slowly closed my eyes. Despite everything, I've actually slept pretty well! No nightmares or anything. I then slowly felt myself drifting to sleep.

I', not sure how long I was out, but I thought I heard a thump in my room a little while later. I couldn't turn my light on, but I thought I saw something in the darkness. It looked like a person slouched over and lifeless.

Suddenly, it glowed a bright yellow and I realized what it was.: that Golden Freddy I had seen on my fourth night. I tried screaming, but it was like it was preventing me from making noise.

Just then, it morphed into what appeared to be...a child! That's when I remembered: there were five missing children. I had only found four.

Before I could think anymore about it, a loud, almost demonic sound blasted in my ears. I still couldn't scream as the image of Golden Freddy stayed frozen in my brain. Even when I closed my eyes, I could still see it, staring menacingly at me with his empty eye sockets.

Finally, after a few seconds, the image disappeared. I then finally heard myself screaming. A few seconds later, Macey charged into the room.

"Are you okay?!" She asked with worry. I looked around the room. No Golden Freddy. No sign of
anyone but her.

"Yeah," I finally told her. "It was just a nightmare."

Five Nights At Freddy's

"Do you need anything?"

"...Some water would be nice."

She then left to get the water. My heart was still racing. I realized right then and there that Golden

Freddy was still haunted. If he even existed. I had never seen signs of him at the pizzeria.

All I knew is that I may have left Freddy Fazbear's Pizza, but Freddy Fazbear's Pizza hasn't left me.

The End

Printed in Great Britain
by Amazon.co.uk, Ltd.,
Marston Gate.